When it's hard to
see

Judith Condon

W
FRANKLIN WATTS
NEW YORK • LONDON • SYDNEY

First published in 1998 by
Franklin Watts,
96 Leonard Street,
London EC2A 4RH

This book was created and produced
for Franklin Watts by Ruth Nason.

Project management: Ruth Nason
Design: Carole Binding
Illustration: Jane Cradock-Watson
Photography: Claire-Maria Cole, Peter Silver.
Consultants: Issy Cole-Hamilton, RNIB;
Beverley Mathias/REACH Resource Centre;
Dr Philip Sawney; William Sawney.

Printed and bound in Belgium

ISBN 0 7496 2997 5

Dewey classification number 617.7

Acknowledgements
The author would like to thank all the
people featured in this book: May Austin,
Lucia Bellini, John Hull, Sally Messer,
Nimesh Shah, Dianne Theakstone, and
pupils and staff at the Royal Blind School,
Edinburgh; Cromer Road School, Barnet;
and Southgate School, Enfield. Also for their
help and advice: Tula Baxter, Jan Blackburn,
John Cheetham, Alison Thomson, and staff of
the RNIB, Action for Blind People, and Look.

The photographs on pages 6t, 13b, 15, 20t
and 20bl were taken by Claire-Maria Cole.
The photographs on pages 14t and 21br
were taken by Peter Silver. Thanks are
also expressed to the following for their
permission to reproduce photographs:
John Birdsall Photography, pages 7t, 12b,
15b, 16tl, 21t, 21bl, 23b; Judith Condon,
page 14b; Eye Ubiquitous (Sean Aidan),
page 26; Richard and Sally Greenhill,
cover, bl; Guide Dogs for the Blind
Association, pages 16tr, 16bl, 17; Getty
Images, page 27; John Hull, page 12t; David
Hurst, page 25; London Transport, page 24;
Photofusion (Christa Stadtler), page 10; RNIB,
pages 6b, 11, 22b, 23t; Science Photo Library
(Blair Seitz), page 13t; Scottish Television,
page 20br; Tony Stone Images (Andy Sacks),
page 22t; Truly
Scrumptious,
cover, br.

Contents

Introduction

The children in this photo enjoyed the day when the Action for Blind People information bus visited their school.

They looked through some special glasses which gave them an idea of what visually impaired people see.

What visually impaired means

Visually impaired is a general term for people who are partially sighted and people who are blind.

Partially sighted people can see 'partly': they see an incomplete or unclear picture of things.

Blind people have no sight, or hardly any. Some may see light from a window or lamp; or the shape of a person, without recognizing the person's face. Only some blind people see nothing at all.

◀ How would you choose and eat a meal if you did not see well?

Using your sight ...

Think how you use your sense of sight all through the day, for instance to:

◆ choose your socks
◆ find the right toothbrush
◆ make your way to school
◆ cross the road safely
◆ read and write
◆ play games
◆ watch television
◆ see your friend smile, and smile back.

Seeing words
We use the word 'see' to mean many things. Think of:

'I see what you mean.' (understand)

'See you tomorrow!' (meet)

'I can't see him being ready in time to catch the train!' (imagine)

Blind people use these expressions just as sighted people do.

... and your other senses

When using your other four senses, you probably often use sight as the decider.

For example, hearing a sound, you turn to see what is making it. Feeling a touch on your arm, you look to check – is it a person, a cat or a spider?!

Tasting or smelling something strange, you look to find out what it is.

Everyday activities

Many everyday activities are harder for someone who is visually impaired. But there are different ways to do things, as you will learn from the people you are going to meet in this book.

Look and find

There is so much to look for and to find in this picture, it's hard to know where to begin!

People are having a day out at the public gardens. Think about how they are using their sense of sight.

Who is enjoying the beautiful flowers? How many signs are there to give people information? Who might be using their eyes to judge what their hands must do?

Can you find a route to the middle of the maze?

What could the people in the picture tell about their surroundings by using their hearing and their senses of touch, taste and smell?

Our eyes help us when we choose, serve and eat food.

We use our sight when we buy things, choose which way to go, and play games.

Plants look beautiful because of their colour and shape, and how they are grouped. They have texture and perfume and may rustle in the breeze.

The gardener needs his sight to sort different coloured plants.

Water is enjoyable to look at and to listen to.

Visual impairment

Visually impaired people come from all backgrounds.

In Britain, a small number of the people who are blind or partially sighted were born with their disability. Others became visually impaired as a result of an accident or an illness.

The largest group of visually impaired people are those whose eyesight fails as they grow older.

◀ Large playing cards are helpful for people who do not see well.

Loss of central vision

Your field of vision is the area you can see. Some people lose sight from one part of their field of vision, for example, the centre.

Loss of central vision mainly affects people over 65. It is caused by damage to the retina (at the back of the eye). Loss of central vision makes it hard to read, and to recognize faces.

Cataracts

In the front part of your eye is a lens. It is usually transparent. But in some people – and animals – the lens becomes misty.

This condition, called a cataract, can usually be treated by an operation.

Patchy or blurred vision

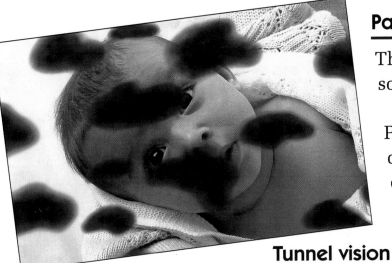

This is how a baby might look to someone with patchy vision.

Patchy vision and blurred vision can be caused by damage to the eye. This can occur in people who have diabetes.

Tunnel vision

Below is how a football match might look to someone with tunnel vision (loss of sight from the edges of their field of vision).

This may be caused by glaucoma, an eye disease that develops in some people over 40. Glaucoma can be treated if it is found early.

River blindness

In central and western Africa, a type of fly that lives in rivers can make people become blind. Over the centuries, millions of people have suffered from 'river blindness'.

The fly's bite infects people with parasites and these invade the eyes.

Now a medicine has been developed to fight river blindness. The plan is to wipe out river blindness by 2007.

Albinism

People with albinism lack some pigments (colours) in their bodies. They have very light coloured hair, skin and eyes. They may have poor vision and a problem seeing colours.

Some people who are visually impaired

Professor John Hull

I am a professor in the University of Birmingham. I give lectures and I write books.

Sometimes I go to speak at conferences (meetings) in other countries.

I read and write using text-to-speech computers (see page 23). My e-mail is set up in speech. I touch-type.

▲ John Hull with two of his sons, Gaby (left) and Josh.

▲ This computer has a voice that can read out the text on the screen.

I live near the University with my wife, Marilyn. Four of my five children still live at home with us. I lost my sight just before Thomas, my second oldest, was born. He is now 17.

I walk to work most days, using my long white cane. Sometimes I get a taxi.

Surprising things happen to you when you are blind. I find it very interesting!

Dianne Theakstone

I am 14 years old
and I live in
Edinburgh.
I go to the Royal
Blind School.

My favourite subjects are
English, Biology and
French. I hope to go on
a trip to Paris next year.

I use Braille for writing and
reading. I also listen to
books on tape.

Braille

Braille is writing that is read by touch.
Letters are made up of combinations
of raised dots.

At Dianne's school, children learn to
read Braille with either hand. They can
then read at the same time as they
use their free hand to do
something else.

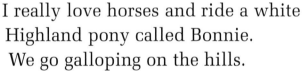

▶ A ClearVision
book has
Braille and
print pages.

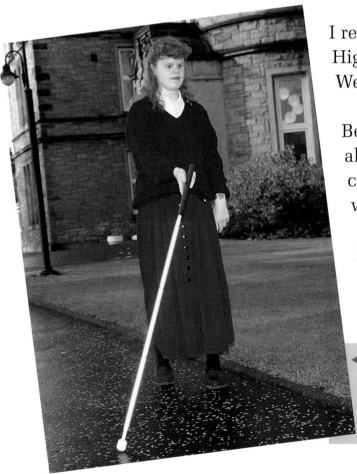

I really love horses and ride a white
Highland pony called Bonnie.
We go galloping on the hills.

Because it's windy up there I can't
always hear the person I'm with, who
calls out if I'm off track. So I wear a
walkie-talkie round my neck.

Riding in an arena is easier. I can
hear the walls! That is, I can sense
where they are.

◀ Dianne knows her way around school
by memory. She uses a long cane
to feel whether the way is clear and
to check for corners and kerbs.

Nimesh Shah

Nimesh was born with a severe eyesight problem.

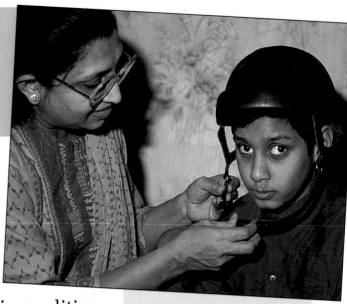

He can see objects if he holds them close to his eyes. He wears glasses but they do not help much. Some days he can see better than others.

Nimesh also has epilepsy, and goes to a special school for children with this condition. He boards (stays overnight) during the week, because the school is some way from home.

▲ Nimesh's disabilities make him likely to fall over. He wears a safety hat when he goes out.

Nimesh loves listening to music, dancing and swimming.

Getting dressed
Some blind people have different-shaped buttons sewn inside their clothes. They learn which shape means which garment, and so can choose the clothes and colours they want to put on.

May Austin

May worked as a travel agent, and then as an antiques dealer.

She loves beautiful things, like paintings, lace and china. But she lost much of her sight when she was ill at the age of 65.

Now in her 80s, May still likes going to the hairdresser, and wearing smart clothes. She loves to meet people and make new friends.

Sally Messer

As Sally wears glasses, some people suppose she is short-sighted or long-sighted. In fact, she has albinism.

She does not see well in dim light. She also has trouble in bright sunlight, especially in autumn when the sun is low in the sky.

By the end of school, her eyes can be very tired and aching.

▲ This close-circuit television (CCTV) enlarges text (placed underneath it) to make it easier to read.

At school, Sally uses a magnifier over the page she is reading. She uses a computer with large text on the screen, and teachers sometimes photocopy work for her in big print.

Sally loves shopping and going to pop concerts. But it's hard to get a place where she can see.

'When you ring up and say you're disabled, they think you're in a wheel-chair,' she explains. 'I get pretty angry about things like that.'

Sally would like to be a manager in the music industry. She also wants to work on behalf of disabled people.

Guide dogs

The Guide Dogs for the Blind Association breeds and trains dogs to serve as the 'eyes' of someone who cannot see.

▼ Labradors and golden retrievers make good guide dogs. They are intelligent and have a gentle manner.

▼ Puppy walkers make sure the puppy becomes used to going on buses and trains.

Puppy walking

When a puppy is six weeks old, it goes to live with a 'puppy walker'.

Puppy walkers are ordinary families who can introduce the puppy to the sights, sounds and smells of town life.

They teach the puppy to walk ahead on its lead, and to obey simple commands.

When the young dog is about one year old, it leaves its 'walker' and goes to a special training centre for about nine months.

At the training centre

At the training centre the young dogs are taught to walk at a steady pace, and to allow room for the person walking with them.

▶ **The dogs learn to guide their trainer safely round obstacles.**

They learn to wait at the kerb, and to cross the road straight when the person they are guiding tells them to. They also learn to disobey the command to cross if it would not be safe.

When they are training, they wear a harness – like the one they will wear when they work as guide dogs.

They learn that they are on duty when the harness is on. When it is off, they can behave just like any pet dog.

Good manners

If you want to pat or talk to a guide dog, always introduce yourself to its owner first.

Don't talk to the dog and not to its owner! To a blind person, this feels like bad manners and can be upsetting. It is as if he or she is invisible.

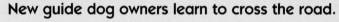

◀ **New guide dog owners learn to cross the road.**

Training the owners

The dogs are introduced to their owners, and the owners are trained to trust and look after their dogs.

People from the age of 16 can apply for a guide dog. They need to be reasonably fit, and have a regular way of life so the dog can join in.

At home

Some of the people who live in these flats are visually impaired.

Look for things they might find helpful, such as:

◆ magnifying glass to read telephone book
◆ lights shining directly on work
◆ lampshades letting out lots of light
◆ tidy room with floor kept clear
◆ magnifying mirror
◆ 'talking' weighing scales
◆ recipes on tape
◆ Braille household bill
◆ large-screen television set
◆ contrasting colours (for example, taps contrasting with bath)

Now can you find things that are not helpful, or even dangerous?

The electricity meter reader is at the door. He will use a password that his company has agreed with the visually impaired person he is calling on. The person will know it is safe to let him in.

Unhelpful: fussy curtains and plants blocking light.

ROSE COURT

Helpful: well-lit white front door.

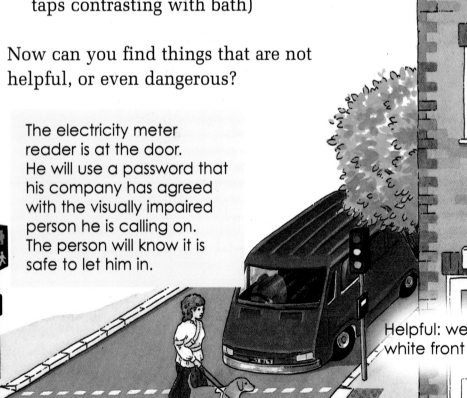

Helpful: plain, light-coloured walls.

Unhelpful: dark, patterned wallpaper.

Helpful: light switch contrasts with wall.

Helpful: basin, bath and toilet in colour that contrasts with walls.

Helpful: cooker controls marked with raised dots.

Helpful: blind that opens right up to let in lots of light.

Helpful: chopping board with different-coloured sides.

19

At school

Left to right are Jodie, Colin, Graham, Katie, Mark and Shaun. They are in Mrs Beckett's class at the Royal Blind School, Edinburgh.

▲ All these children have a visual impairment. Mark, in dark glasses, is photo-phobic – this means that his eyes hurt in bright light.

The school has about 120 pupils, aged 3 to 19, from all over Scotland and northern England. Some of the children – including Katie, Jodie, Mark and Shaun – board during the week.

Others, like Colin and Graham, come from home each day.

◀ Colin has a good light close to his work.

Extra activities

The older pupils at the Royal Blind School put on a theatre production each year. Here they are in *Oklahoma!*

Each summer, the school takes part in a swimming gala, competing with other schools in the area.

Mainstream schools

Most children who are visually impaired go to mainstream (ordinary) schools.

Like other pupils with special needs, they may have extra support in some lessons.

At an 'Early Start Nursery' for visually impaired children, Guy is encouraged to investigate using his sense of touch.

Also, a 'mobility teacher' may come to help them develop confidence and independence in getting around inside and outside the school buildings.

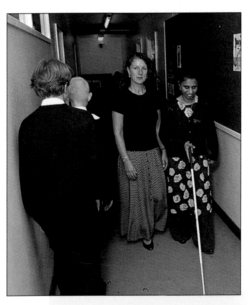

It can be hard for a visually impaired pupil if other people make him or her feel different from everyone else. Good friends are important.

▲ A mobility teacher helps Rukhsana learn the way around her school.

Noisy writing!

Shaun, at the Royal Blind School, explains that writing with a Brailler can be noisy.

'If you press too softly, the dots are too soft and you can't read it. If you press hard, the dots come up nice and sharp. There's also a bell that tells you when it's got six spaces left on the paper. I'm surprised it doesn't hurt Mrs Beckett's head when we're all working at once!'

Writing Braille

Children learn to write Braille, using a machine called a Brailler. They also use computers that print Braille. Lucia (right) goes to a mainstream school and uses a Brailler to make notes.

At work

People who
are visually
impaired work
in a variety of
ordinary and
unusual jobs.

▶ **A blind worker
on a computer
assembly line.**

Judge John Wall

John Wall is a judge. He doesn't
think that not seeing makes
him less good at his job.
He points out that people
often try to use the way
they look to trick judges!

In his spare time, John plays
chess. He posts his 'moves' in
Braille to his opponents. He is
known for his fantastic memory.

He also works hard for visually
impaired people all over Europe.
He is Chairman of the Royal
National Institute for the Blind.

Employers

Many employers
recognize that visually
impaired and other
disabled people work
as well as anyone,
if they have the right
equipment and training.

But some employers do
not give disabled workers
a chance. Because of this,
it can be hard for visually
impaired people to get
good jobs.

There are now laws to
ensure that disabled
workers are treated fairly.

The Royal National Institute for the Blind (RNIB) and other organizations work to increase opportunities for people with visual impairment. They offer support and advice. RNIB colleges train people in work skills.

People need support when they start a job, or when they are adjusting to loss of sight during their working life.

▲ The man is using a scanner (on his right). A synthesized voice reads out the page of the book in the scanner.

Personal computers

Text on a computer screen can be made very large. It can also be printed large.

Computers and printers can be adapted to print Braille.

Many computers have speech synthesizers, which read out the text on the screen.

Some computers can be worked by speaking at them. This is called 'speech recognition'.

A scanner can be joined to a computer. The page of a book in the scanner appears on the computer screen. The writing can then be enlarged, or the computer can read out the page. This is how John Hull (see page 12) reads books.

◀ What equipment can you see on Lorraine's desk?

More examples of useful equipment

◆ Mini tape-recorders, for making notes
◆ Calculators with large print on the keys
◆ 'Talking' calculators and dictionaries
◆ Telephones that can store phone numbers in their memory

Getting around

▲ On modern railway stations the edge of the platform is marked by a change of surface.

Clear the way!

Litter could cause a visually impaired person to fall.

Other dangers are branches sticking out from front gardens and cars parked partly on the pavement.

Many people who are blind learn to find their way to places, by feeling with their long cane.

Different surfaces underfoot are helpful. The feel of the pavement changes at a pedestrian crossing.

Changes of floor surface can be used indoors, for example to show the way to the lift or stairs.

Warning sounds and announcements

At this unusual bus stop information is displayed about when the bus will arrive. You can also press a button to hear the information. The large black button is clear for partially sighted people to see.

In trains with sliding doors a sound warns when the doors are about to open or close. In buses, trains and lifts, there may be spoken announcements of what the next stop will be.

Where else do you think there should be spoken announcements?

Maps and timetables

Many bus companies provide enlarged maps and timetables. London Transport supplies large-print and Braille versions of the Underground map, and 'talking' timetables and station guides, on tape.

VIPER

VIPER stands for Visually Impaired Personal Electronic Reader – an invention by Mark Wyman, for use in supermarkets.

It is a hand-held scanner. Customers point it at the bar code on an item, and a synthesized voice describes the item.

Airlines

Airlines may provide a helper to accompany visually impaired passengers through the airport and onto their plane.

How to help

Many blind people appreciate help to cross the road, or to find a particular place. But always ask first: 'Can I help at all?'

If the answer is yes, ask how the person would like to be guided, and where to. Most people prefer to hold your arm, just above your elbow.

Walk half a pace ahead, so the person can tell from your movements when to turn or stop.

A blind adventurer

David Hurst, who is blind, has climbed Mont Blanc, run over 30 marathons, and taken a jungle survival course in Borneo.

In August 1997, while swimming in the sea in North Wales, he heard a surf-boarder in trouble. He swam towards the sound, deciding not to say that he was blind, and brought the man to safety.

▶ Visually impaired people take part in many kinds of sport. David Hurst is a champion waterskier.

Famous people

David Blunkett

David Blunkett was born in 1947. At age 4, he went as a boarder to a school for blind children. He learned Braille and also had fun playing cricket, bike-riding and go-karting.

After university he became a teacher, and then a Member of Parliament. In 1997 he was given the important position of Secretary of State for Education and Employment.

David has written a book about his life, called *On a Clear Day*. It also describes his guide dogs.

◀ **David and his guide dog, Lucy.**

Catherine Cookson

One of the biggest-selling authors of all time, Catherine Cookson (born in 1906) writes stories about everyday life in the part of northeast England where she grew up. In her nineties, she has become almost blind, but goes on producing new books every year.

Johannes Kepler

Born in Germany in 1571, Kepler had smallpox as a child, which left him visually impaired. He studied mathematics and became a great astronomer, discovering laws about the orbits of the planets.

Hellos and goodbyes

When you meet people you know who are blind:

- ◆ say their name or lightly touch their arm, so that they know you are talking to them
- ◆ say who you are, in case they do not recognize your voice
- ◆ tell them when you are about to leave. Otherwise they may go on talking, thinking you are still there.

Helen Keller

Born in 1880 in the USA, Helen Keller became permanently blind and deaf as a result of illness when a baby.

Anne Sullivan, who had been blind herself, taught Helen the names of objects by pressing the shapes of letters onto her palm. Later, Helen learned Braille and gained a university degree. She wrote books and toured the world.

Ved Mehta

An illness when he was 3 left Ved totally blind. At 15, he went to blind school in the USA. Later he studied at Oxford University, England. He has been a writer since he was 20. His books tell about his childhood in India and his Hindu family.

John Milton

The great English poet Milton (1608-74) went blind at the age of 44. He wrote his famous long poem, *Paradise Lost*, in his head, then said it aloud for his daughter to write down.

▶ Stevie Wonder, in 1965.

Stevie Wonder

American Stevland Morris was born blind in 1950. He was given the stage name Little Stevie Wonder at age 10 – when he already played harmonica, drums, organ and piano. He has had many hit records, including 'I Just Called to Say I Love You'.

Stevie has also helped black people campaign for their rights.

Glossary

albinism

inherited condition where the body lacks certain pigments. It affects the way light acts on the eyes.

blind

About 18 in 100 visually impaired people are classed as totally blind. Most of these can distinguish between light and dark. In Britain people may be entered on an official register of blind people, and this entitles them to certain benefits and/or services.

Braille

a system of writing using raised dots. The number of people who use Braille is quite small. To use it you need to develop a good sense of touch. This can be hard for people who lose their sight in later life.

diabetes

a disease which causes the blood to contain too much

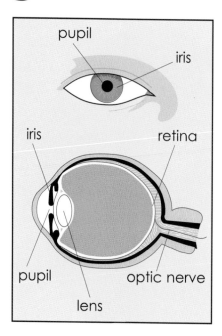

glucose (sugar). If not controlled by diet and tablets or daily injections, diabetes can result in damage to the eye. The damage can eventually cause blindness.

e-mail

electronic mail: messages sent from from one computer to another.

epilepsy

problem of incorrect signals in the brain, which can cause a person to become unconscious and make his or her arms and legs jerk.

Light rays from an object pass through the pupil and the lens of your eye and are focused on the retina. Messages about the light rays travel along the optic nerve to your brain, and you see the object.

field of vision

the area you can see ahead when your eyes are not moving.

partially sighted

a general term that describes loss of vision that is less severe than blindness.

retina

area inside the back of the eyeball, onto which light coming through the pupil is focused.

touch-type

type without needing to look at the keys.

visually impaired

general term for people who are blind or partially sighted.

Useful addresses

Action for Blind People
14-16 Verney Road,
London SE16 3DZ
tel 0171 732 8771
(sends information bus to
schools by arrangement)

ClearVision
Linden Lodge School,
61 Princes Way,
London SW19
(produces books with both
Braille and printed text)

**Guide Dogs for the Blind
Association**
Hillfields,
Burghfield Common,
Reading RG7 3YG
tel 01734 835555
fax 01734 835211

**London Transport Unit for
Disabled Passengers**
172 Buckingham Palace Rd,
London SW1W 9TN
tel 0171 918 3176

John Hull (see page 12) has
written a fascinating book:
*On Sight and Insight, a
Journey into the World of
Blindness* (One World, 1997).

Look (the National
Federation of Families
with Visually Impaired
Children)
Chairman: Mrs Tula Baxter,
25 Newlands Avenue,
Thames Ditton,
Surrey KT7 0HD
tel/fax 0181 224 0735

REACH (National Resource
Centre for Children with
Reading Difficulties),
Wellington House,
Wellington Road,
Wokingham,
Berkshire RG40 2AG
tel 0118 989 1101
fax 0118 979 0989

**Royal National Institute
for the Blind (RNIB)**
Education and Employment
Information Service,
224 Great Portland Street,
London W1N 6AA
tel 0171 388 1266

IN AUSTRALIA

**Blind Vision
Information Line**
Free Call 1800 331 000

Papers, books and films

The Talking Newspaper
Association records 200
national newspapers
and many magazines
onto audio cassette
or computer disk.

The RNIB employs
actors to make tape
recordings of books.

The RNIB supplies
videos of films with
a voice describing the
scene and what is
happening when there
is no dialogue.

Royal Blind Society
4 Mitchell Road, Enfield,
NSW 2136, Sydney
tel 61 2 9334 3333

**Royal Institute for Deaf
and Blind Children**
361-5 North Rocks Road,
North Rocks,
NSW 2151, Sydney
tel 61 2 9871 1233

Index